Big Bill and Buddies
Book Two

Brendon Mouse's Big Idea to Save the Bad Bird Bunch

Written and Illustrated by
Greg Watkins

PELICAN PUBLISHING COMPANY
Gretna 2007

In loving memory of my nephew, Eugene

I want to thank my parents, brothers, and sisters for their support. I want to thank Bob and Kathy for all they have done for me, and Bob, Brendon, and D.J. for the great memories. I would like to thank my goddaughter, Sarah, and all my fellow Marines and veterans. I want to thank some very special friends who helped me through my illnesses: Father Dave, Sister Marietta, Father Frank, and Father John. I would especially like to thank Jenniffer and Eric for helping make this a great book. I am grateful to you all as my life would not be as full without you.

First edition, 2005
First Pelican edition, 2007

ISBN-13: 978-1-58980-449-4
LCCN 2005-921867

Designed by Jenniffer Julich, Jnnffr Productions
Composition and layout by Eric Tufford

Printed in Singapore
Published by Pelican Publishing Company, Inc.
1000 Burmaster Street, Gretna, Louisiana 70053

"Whew! This Has Been A Crazy Day,"

said Brendon Mouse
as he scratched
his little head.

"Boy, you can sure say *that* again,"
added Bill, *the* Big Beaked, Big Bellied Bird.

"Whew! This Has Been A Crazy Day,"

Brendon Mouse replied with a giggle.
"Brendon, you are so silly," laughed Bob Cat.

1

"I can't believe I was almost eaten by an alligator!" Bill exclaimed. "Yeah," said DJ Dog, "I don't know why that **Bad Bird Bunch** wanted to push you into the mouth of an alligator." "Maybe because **they are bullies**," grumbled Bob Cat.

"We've got to go help the Bad Bird Bunch get away from that alligator. He was chasing them pretty fast," said Brendon Mouse.

"Why Brendon?" asked Bob Cat.

"When somebody's in trouble, you have to help. It's the only thing to do," replied Brendon.

"He's right," said Bartholomew Worm.

"Let's go help them!"

3

"I'm a little nervous about helping them," said Bill.

"Don't you want to help?" asked DJ Dog.

Bill replied, "I do, but I'm scared of the hungry alligator."

"It's okay to be afraid sometimes. I'm scared too, but **I have a good friend** that I know will want to help," announced Brendon Mouse.

"What's wrong with girls?" asked Brendon.

"Nothing's wrong with girls.

But if we're scared, won't a girl
be scared too?" asked DJ Dog.

"Girls can do anything boys can do. Besides,
she's not your average girl," laughed Brendon.

"What do you mean?" asked Bill.

"Ellie is the kind of person who would
help anyone that asked her, even if she
was scared. When we first met, she
was scared
of little
old me.

6

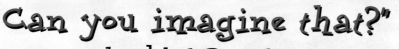

Can you imagine that?"

chuckled Brendon.

"Why would anyone be afraid of a mouse?" wondered Bob Cat.

"We need to find your friend now, so we can help the Bad Bird Bunch," added Bartholomew Worm,

"Let's Go!"

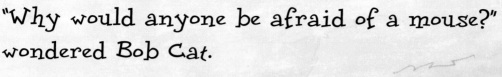

7

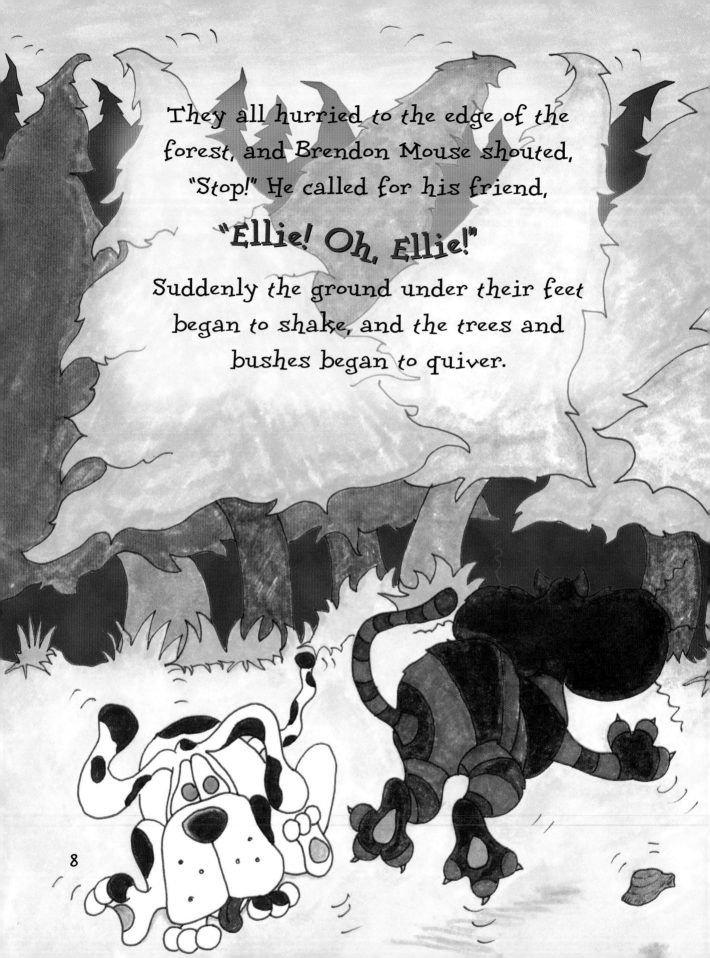

They all hurried to the edge of the
forest, and Brendon Mouse shouted,
"Stop!" He called for his friend,

"Ellie! Oh, Ellie!"

Suddenly the ground under their feet
began to shake, and the trees and
bushes began to quiver.

8

With a loud crash, Brendon's
not so small friend appeared.

Brendon's buddies were speechless
as they stared up at her.

**"This is my friend,
Ellie Funt!"**
Brendon said proudly.

9

"She's... She's...
an elephant,"
stumbled DJ Dog.

"Let me be the first
to say hello, Ellie.
I'm Bob Cat," he said,
introducing himself.

Brendon finished
the introductions.

Ellie replied in her
cheerful way, "I sure am
glad to meet you all!

**Any friend
of Brendon's
is a friend
of mine!"**

10

The friends told Ellie all
about the Bad Bird Bunch
and the hungry alligator.

"Hop on
and I'll give
you a ride.

We'll find that Bad Bird
Bunch!" she cried.

It wasn't
long before they
**spotted the
Bad Bird Bunch.**

From the top of a big hill,
the friends saw the
alligator standing at
the bottom of a tree.

Bill Bird, DJ Dog, and
Bob Cat jumped off
Ellie's back and ran
ahead of the others.

Bob Cat yelled, "Stop, you big old alligator!"

"Yeah," added Bill, **"leave those birds alone!"**

The alligator was so surprised he almost jumped out of his skin.

13

But when he
turned around
to see who was
yelling, he only
laughed and asked,

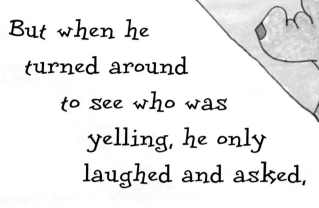

"Why do you care about these birds?

They wanted me to eat
you, the Big Beaked, Big
Bellied Bird named Bill!
You should run along
before I turn you
all into dinner."

14

The Bad Bird Bunch heard
what was going on and shouted,
"No, don't leave!
We're sorry for what we did!"

Bill replied,

"I forgive you.

Come on down from
that tree, you guys."

"Now, wait just one minute,"
the alligator demanded.
"Who do you think you are?

I'm in charge here!

If anyone's getting down,
they're getting down right
into my stomach!

"HA! HA! HA!"
laughed the alligator.

But the
alligator
was so busy
laughing
he didn't see
who had
stepped up
behind him.

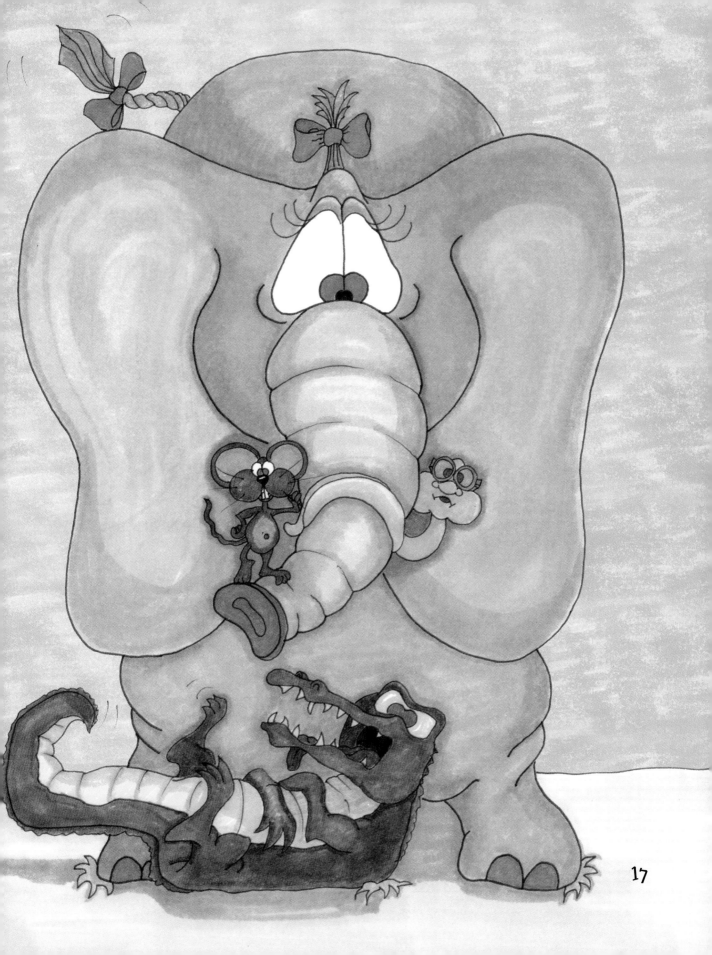

17

18

"Howdy, little alligator. My name is
Ellie Funt. What's yours?" she asked.
Slowly the alligator turned around, and
Ellie Funt was standing there with
Brendon Mouse and Bartholomew Worm
on top of her head.
With a big gulp he answered,
"Cooper. Cooper Gator's my name."

"Would you like a lift up into the tree?
You weren't trying to eat somebody,
were you, little fellow?" Ellie questioned.
Cooper Gator nervously stumbled over his answer,
"I um... Well er... Oh yeah... I was just
telling your friends **I was leaving."**

"That sounds like a great idea. It's not nice to be picking on anybody, is it, Cooper?" Ellie asked.

"Nope, I sure wouldn't want to scare anyone around here," Cooper answered. "I *think* I'll be going now." So with a swish of his tail, a turn of his head, and a cloud of dust,

Cooper Gator ran away as fast as he could go.

20

With Cooper Gator gone, Bully Bird and his bunch flew down from the tree. Everyone was laughing and cheering!

21

"Thanks for all your help," said Bully Bird happily. "We really are sorry for being so mean to you all."

"Yeah, it's not very fun to be bad," said Blue Bird. "We always thought we were better than everyone else. But after seeing how you all are friends, we realize being bullies isn't cool."

"Yes, I think Blue's right," agreed Bully Bird. "When everybody is afraid of you, it's hard to make any friends."

23

"I know what you mean," replied Ellie.
"Some people are afraid of me because I'm
so big. None of the smaller folks would ever
ask me to play because they were scared.

Brendon Mouse was the first
little person that ever came up to me
and asked if I wanted to play, and
we have been buddies ever since.
So you see, no matter if you are
big or small, weak or strong,
you always need friends."

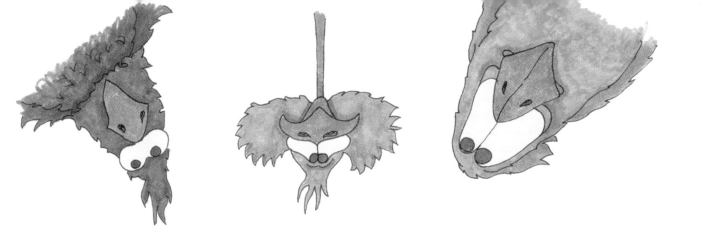

"You know what, Ellie?" asked Bully Bird.

"I never realized how lonely I was until

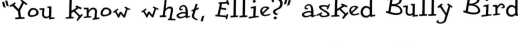

I saw how kind and friendly these guys could be," said Bully Bird, shaking his head sadly.

"Is Bully Bird your real name?"
asked Bill.

"No, my real name is Tracy,"
Bully Bird said quietly.

"I changed my name to Bully Bird so
I would sound tough. But now I know
I should just be myself."

"I think we've all learned a
great lesson today!"
Ellie trumpeted.

27

"Now *there's* only one more problem,"
said Tracy. "If we're not the
Bad Bird Bunch anymore,
what do we call ourselves?"

"How about buddies?" offered Brendon Mouse.

Learn how important true buddies can be,
as we all wait for the excitement
we'll find in book three!

"Ellie's Extra Exciting, Enormous Secret Dream"